PLOTS & PARANOIA

MRS. POMOLO INVESTIGATES

DONNA MUSE

CLICK HERE to Join our Reader's Club and to Receive Tica House Updates!

https://cozymystery.subscribemenow.com/

CONTENTS

[1]

AT THE BEGINNING of the year, Geneva Pomolo and her housemate, Iris Reeves, decided they needed to do more running.

Both made the decision for different reasons. Iris had been asked out on a date by a nephew of Paul Anka, a man in his fifties who sang jazzy songs in the style of Michael Bublé or his more famous uncle. Pulling an old dress out of the closet, she was dismayed to find she could no longer fit into it. Geneva's resolution was occasioned by a visit to the doctor, who informed her she had gained ten pounds over the Christmas holidays (for which Geneva blamed Iris), and that "if you don't start following a consistent workout regimen, you may not live to see sixty-five."

"I don't know what more he wants," Geneva fumed when she returned home from her checkup on the first day of the year. "Are we not the most active of women? Have I not sprained ankles and broken bones falling off roofs?"

"Personally, I don't think excess weight is your problem," said Iris, who was seated at the kitchen table eating a dough-covered hot dog on a stick. "Given the pummeling your body has been through in the past three or four years—getting clobbered and shot at and pushed into cold rivers and almost dying in a fire—it's a miracle you're not in *worse* shape."

"I think you look rather nice," said Geneva's gentleman friend, George Wilson, who was seated on the living room sofa reading a book about Jewish life in the Middle Ages. No matter how much weight Geneva gained, George would find her irresistibly good-looking.

"Thank you, dear," said Geneva, blushing slightly. "But what if Dr. Spaceman is right? I would be doing a disservice to myself and to the community if I died because I failed to exercise properly. I almost think—"

She fell silent, watching Iris nibble at her hot dog with a gloomy expression. "You know, Iris," she said, "it wouldn't kill *you* to take better care of yourself."

Iris set down the hot dog with an indignant stare. "What does that mean, exactly?"

"You remember a few Christmases ago when George started on that diet and exercise regimen. He's been eating better, losing weight, his face looks like a baby orange with a smooth peeling. Meanwhile we're sitting here eating greasy rotisserie chickens, fried calamari, chicken fried steaks with brown gravy—"

"Not all those things at once, surely," said Iris.

"No, but in a typical week it's alarming the amount and kinds of food we put away. You won't normally hear me saying this, but I think we ought to follow George's example. We could be adding years to our lives if we made this the year we started taking better care of ourselves."

"I'll get right on that," said Iris dryly. "Just as soon as I finish these tater tots."

But when Iris learned her co-workers in the water department had resolved to eat better and exercise more in the coming year, she began to wonder if maybe Geneva was right. Feeling a bit foolish, she went out and bought a track suit, a pair of running shorts, and a tracker to measure her jogging times. Over a light dinner of kale and potato soup, she and Geneva drew up a jogging schedule in which they ran together two mornings during the week and on Saturdays. "But please can we treat ourselves to a big breakfast when we finish our Saturday runs?" she asked. "I need an omelet incentive to keep me motivated."

"We can have *one* big brunch at the end of the week," said Geneva. "George, you're welcome to meet up with us."

"Won't that just undo all the progress you made during the week?" George pointed out.

"All right, then you can stay home," Geneva replied.

On the following Tuesday at dawn, Geneva and Iris woke early and set out together on their first run. They jogged through their suburb of Turtle Creek to River Ranch Road, a major road running east-west through Wrangler's Hill. It was dotted with shopping plazas smelling tantalizingly of grease and salt and potatoes. It was a gray morning in, and snow was coming down in light flurries and piling up in drifts along the streets and sidewalks. Two or three crows sat perched in a row along a power line, sleepily ruffling their feathers as if just emerging from winter hibernation.

"I don't know how much longer I can do this, Gen," said Iris, in a voice like Frodo's in Mordor.

"Iris, we've been jogging for ten minutes," Geneva pointed out. "My doctor says once you've been doing it for a few weeks, you start to develop stamina. It gets easier."

"If I can make it till then," muttered Iris.

"Try thinking of other things. What are your five favorite Agatha Christie novels?"

Iris slowed her pace, ostensibly to consider this. "That's a hard one. I tend to like the fun ones with a bit of romance, where the guy wins the girl in the end or vice versa. I don't know, the one on the plane maybe? I love all the Marples."

Geneva listed hers; she tended toward the darker and more introspective. "*The Murder of Roger Ackroyd*, obviously... *Endless Night* is criminally underrated... I like when she stops trying to write clever plots and focuses on character. She understands the criminal mind so thoroughly, it's eerie..."

She shivered. The wind was beginning to pick up. Agreeing that the weather was only going to get worse, and there was no sense in subjecting themselves to further misery, they stopped at the Waffle House in Food-a-Rama Plaza, where they both ordered coffee and a single hard-boiled egg.

Gladys Culpepper, a friend from church, was on morning duty, her cat eyeglasses glinting in the overhead fluorescent lights. She hummed cheerfully to herself as she poured their coffee.

"What's with you?" asked Iris, somewhat rudely. "You seem awfully chipper for seven in the morning."

"Life will do that to you," said Gladys, rather mysteriously. "Let's just say some very bad things that have been going on for a long time finally ended this weekend."

Geneva and Iris exchanged looks as she returned to the kitchen. "Did she kill a guy?" whispered Iris.

Gladys emerged a second later carrying several small containers of creamer on a tray. "Gladys, you can't just leave us hanging like this," said Geneva. "It's bad storytelling, for one."

"You never really stopped being a literature teacher, did you?" asked Gladys, smiling. "Well, if you must know... there's been a curse over our family for a long time, and yesterday after church, a man came to our house and lifted it."

Geneva wasn't sure how she felt about this. "Lifted? How?"

"His name is Christabel Dollar," said Gladys, "and he specializes in exorcisms, generational curses and whatnot. I told him I've been having serious back pains for three years and the doctors weren't able to fix it. Twice our car has been broken into and the radio stolen. He asked if he could go into our bedroom and after he had been meditating for a few minutes he said, 'There's a cursed object in this room. A witch doctor broke in and planted it here to bring misery to you and your loved ones.' Then he lifted the mattress and what do you think he found?"

"No telling," said Geneva.

"Not a clue," said Iris.

Gladys leaned forward and said quietly, *"It was a rubber snake."*

"A rubber snake?" Geneva repeated.

"So, not a real one?" said Iris.

"No, it was almost worse." Gladys shivered in disgust. "The witch doctors, they have these rituals where they place demons into everyday household objects, and then they sneak those objects into people's homes. Then those people wonder why their kids are sick, their spouses are in prison, they've suddenly come down with cancer—"

"Can witch doctors *do* all that?" cried Iris, aghast.

"You wouldn't believe the things they can do," said Gladys in a conspiratorial whisper. "If not for Christabel I... I don't know what I'd have done."

She went back to the counter, leaving Geneva and Iris to stare silently at their mugs.

"I'd like to meet this Christabel fellow," said Geneva after a long pause. "How much money is he charging for these 'deliverance' sessions?"

"But he found a *snake*," said Iris, stirring a package of sweetener into her coffee. "I'd love for someone to explain how it came to be under their mattress."

"Most likely it was left there years ago, and she forgot about it," Geneva replied. "He seized on the strangest thing he could find in the room and claimed it was full of 'demonic energies.'"

"Is her back really feeling better, I wonder," said Iris, gazing across the diner at Gladys. "By the way, I'm afraid I'll have to postpone our jogging session on Saturday. There's a runner's event I wanted to go to."

"Runner's event?" said Geneva, sounding impressed. "That seems a little ambitious."

"Oh, it's nothing like that," Iris said with a light laugh. "It should be illegal to put me on a track in front of an audience at this age. "No, Regina Baldwin is coming to Wrangler's. She's going to be emceeing a marathon."

The tone of her voice made it clear that Geneva ought to recognize the name. "I must be losing my memory in my old age; remind me who this is?"

"Regina Baldwin," said Iris unhelpfully. "The famous runner? Beloved fitness guru, featured in *O Magazine*?"

"Oh, Regina. Right."

"Anyway, she's flying in on Friday," said Iris, "and she'll be recording an episode of her wellness podcast in Bartleby Hall for an audience of about five hundred women. Then on

Saturday she's hosting the marathon, and on Sunday, she's being presented an award by the Jewish Women of Wrangler's Hill."

This rundown of Regina's itinerary left Geneva with the distinct impression that Iris had been charting her every movement for months. "I'd like to go, if you're going," she said. "How much are the tickets?"

"They're free if you go with me." Reaching into her purse, Iris flashed a pair of blue tickets. "Mr. Rolls Royce was supposed to go with me, but he bailed when I had to postpone our date because of the dress incident."

"Good riddance to him, then," said Geneva. "Maybe watching a marathon will motivate us to participate in the next one."

"You're a real jokester," said Iris, cutting her egg in half. "If I even manage to walk back to the house, I'll consider it a win."

"Iris, we live three blocks away," Geneva pointed out.

"Like I said," Iris replied, and went on eating her egg.

$$[\ 2\ ]$$

OVER THE NEXT FEW DAYS, the two women began dieting in earnest. Iris went to the supermarket on Wednesday after work and returned home with bags full of tofu, cabbage, ramen, kale, cauliflower, and various foods that looked like meat, but on closer inspection were revealed to be made of plants or soy. "They've gotten these 'impossible foods' down to an art now," said Iris. "If I told you this was real chicken nuggets, you wouldn't be able to tell the difference."

"I'm pretty sure I could tell the difference," said Geneva, shoving a bag of cranberries into the bottom drawer of the refrigerator.

For dinner that night, Iris made a curried cauliflower quinoa salad while Geneva prepared a pull-apart garlic-cheese bread so appetizing they both felt a little guilty eating it. George was on his way home from work; he had recently landed a gig as a receptionist at the Wrangler's Hill Jazz Club.

"Tell me this," said Geneva as she pulled the bread into pieces: "what are the cleverest *murders* in Agatha Christie's novels?"

Iris frowned apprehensively. "I don't know, I guess the one in *Death Comes for the Archbishop*—"

"You must be thinking of another book," said Geneva, setting the plate with the bread on it down on the table. "*Death Comes for the Archbishop* is a novel by Willa Cather. And a fantastic read, I might."

"Well, what's the one where the villain slowly undermines the foundations of an old manor home, removing one brick at a time, until finally the whole building topples and kills his horrible, sadistic wife? That's *Crooked House*, right?"

"No, *Crooked House* is the one—I don't want to spoil it if you've not read it—"

"Isn't there one where a woman is killed by a falling house?"

"No, you must be thinking of *Midsomer Murders*." Geneva paused, staring intently at her partner. "Wait, how many Christies have you actually read?"

Iris turned away her face. "Promise you won't make fun of me—"

Geneva stifled a gasp. "Iris. No."

"Yeah... I might have read the one about the island, years ago... but I've never gotten into Christie, I'm sorry. You're welcome to kick me out of the business if you'd like. I was hoping this would never come up."

"But when we were running the other day—"

"The ladies in the office *love* Agatha," said Iris, gazing intently at her nails, "and between them and you, I've picked up enough to be able to carry on a conversation."

Geneva couldn't get over this. "Iris, how can you aspire to be a mystery novelist and yet you've never read Agatha Christie?"

"I *do* read mysteries," said Iris, "just not hers. I like my novels to have strong characters who feel like real, flesh-and-blood human beings. As far as I can tell, Agatha's a great plotter but a terrible writer of people. All her characters feel like pawns being shoved across a chessboard. I read the island one and never felt the need to read another one."

Geneva shook her head; she seemed to be reconsidering her entire friendship with Iris. "Maybe you made the wrong resolution. Forget about dieting; we need to get you—"

But she never finished the sentence, for at that moment they both heard a great noise from the street in front of the house, as if a hundred voices were all shouting together, chanting in chorus: "RED, BLACK, WHITE, BROWN — NO MORE CONVICTS IN OUR TOWN."

"What on earth is going on out there?" asked Geneva, running toward the window. She let out an oath as she gazed across the lawn to the house next door. "Iris, you have to come see this."

Setting down the salad bowl, Iris strode to the window. A crowd of about fifty people had gathered on the front lawn of the next house over, where lived their friend Hilda Bobrick, a twenty-something teacher with some decidedly old-fashioned views on television, popular culture, and the criminal justice system. Hilda stood at the front of the crowd speaking into a microphone, waving her arms like a conductor leading an orchestra. From this Geneva deduced that it had been she who had organized the chant.

"What are they all yelling about?" said Iris, perturbed. "Who's putting convicts in Wrangler's Hill?"

Geneva wasn't sure she wanted to know the answer; this had all the makings of a carefully orchestrated social panic. "I suppose we had better go over there and find out."

Grabbing her coat from the coat rack, she opened the door and strode out before Iris could protest.

All up and down the street, porch lights were flickering on and heads were peering through doors and out of windows at the commotion that Hilda was rousing up. Geneva found the little group standing pressed close together, several of them holding signs that read "KEEP CRIMINALS OUT OF OUR COMMUNITY" and "LAWBREAKERS MUST BE PUNISHED TO THE FULLEST EXTENT."

When she saw Geneva coming, Hilda's face brightened, and she motioned for the chanting to subside. Seemingly energized by the support of the crowd, she raised her lips to the megaphone.

"They can try to arrest us," she said. "They can haul us away in handcuffs, like they did to me once before on this very lawn. But we won't be silenced." There was a smattering of cheers. "They can try to shut us up, but they will fail. Because we live in a free country, where we can say whatever the *heck* we want." (She placed slightly too much emphasis on the word *heck*, as if she had never said it before). "They can put their boots on our necks, but they can't stop our mouths."

More cheering at this. "Hilda, what's all this about?" asked Iris, who had been watching the proceedings with matronly disapproval. "Why is everyone so worked up?"

Rather than answering directly, Hilda continued to address the crowd. "There are some folks who are only just now joining us," she said, "who may not be aware that the police intend to release a dangerous maniac and attempted murderer into this community. Mordecai Whistler served ten years in state prison for kidnapping his own wife. He's a menace to the rule of law, and in a just society—one where men were still men—"

"That's right," said a little man to Geneva's left, in a faint voice.

"In a just society," Hilda went on, clearly relishing the attention, "the name of Mordecai Whistler would never again darken the light of day. In a matter of days, Mr. Whistler will be moving into a house at the end of this street, where he'll have free rein to terrorize your wives and torment your children. If you care about law and order, if you care about justice—"

"Dear Lord, this is insane," Iris muttered.

"You'll join me in letting the police know we don't *want* a murderer in this neighborhood. We don't want a kidnapper living here. What do we want? We want this law-breaking scum to go back to the abyss where he came from. We want all miscreants to remove themselves from our carefully tended lawns and stop bothering decent, respectable, law-abiding folks."

Most of the people standing in front of her cheered at this; it was clear that Hilda's speech had left an impression. Only one person—a man in his late twenties with a pale face, wearing a black beanie—stood looking on with a sour expression.

"I hate to ruin anyone's party," he said, "but what are you all expecting to do about this? He served his time and was released. The parole board evidently decided he could be safely admitted back into society. And last I heard, you can't legally prevent a neighbor from renting or buying a house."

"Emmett, why are you defending a convicted criminal?" asked Hilda, and several of the others murmured their agreement. "We have a responsibility, as citizens, to defend our children from evil-doers—"

"Do we?" said the man named Emmett. "I thought we had a responsibility to follow the law, not whip up mobs for the sake of harassing private citizens."

There was an eruption of booing and hissing; clearly Emmett was not interested in saying whatever would make him more popular.

"I think Emmett has a point, though," came a woman's voice a few paces behind him. She stepped forward into the dusky half-light, revealing one of the most oddly dressed women Geneva had ever seen. She wore an old-fashioned maroon hat that wouldn't have looked out of place on a Jazz Era-flapper, and around her neck hung an enormous pink feather boa. Despite the forbidding weather, she was fashionably dressed in a black sleeveless dress that exposed both her shoulders.

"I'm sorry, who are you?" asked Hilda, understandably flummoxed by the appearance of this strange woman.

"Freya Watt," said the woman. "I live in Heringay Hills. Personally, I think we should have more tolerance for the incarcerated. Many of them were framed by the FBI as part of an organized push to put all right-thinking people in prison."

Nobody knew quite what to say to this. She spoke in such a matter-of-fact way that if someone wasn't listening very carefully, they might not realize that what she was saying was utterly deranged.

"Freya, listen," said Emmett, "I appreciate your wanting to help me—"

"No, it's true," said Freya brightly. "I learned all about it online, from the most reliable website. Back in the 1980s, the FBI was selling these nativity sets with bags of heroin hidden inside the mangers, and then when people bought them, the feds would swoop down onto their homes and arrest them for drug possession. Thousands upon thousands of men and women went to prison whose only crime was buying a nativity set for Christmas."

"I don't think that's true," said Geneva slowly. "In fact, I feel pretty confident in saying that *none* of that is true."

"Of course, it's true," said Freya, peering over at her with wide, solemn eyes. "Why else do you think no one celebrates Christmas anymore?"

"Look, all I'm saying," said Emmett, clearly wishing to distance himself from his defender, "is that we are a nation of laws. Laws punish criminals so that mobs don't have to—"

"Which is why," said Hilda, eager to make herself once again the center of attention, "I say we march down to the police station together on this coming Saturday and make our voices HEARD. We won't relent until Mr. Whistler has found new lodgings, far, far from here. We won't be bullied by well-meaning policemen who want us to put our heads down and accept the repatriation of irredeemables into our midst."

Everyone cheered at this—everyone except the two women, and Freya, and Emmett. Clenching her left hand into a fist and raising it high in the air, Hilda shouted, "Saturday. Noon. Meet me at this spot and we will march on the station together. This is a battle for the souls of your wives and daughters, but together WE WILL PREVAIL."

"WE WILL PREVAIL," the crowd cried, as Hilda pumped her fist jubilantly into the air. "WE WILL PREVAIL. WE WILL PREVAIL."

Iris and Geneva exchanged troubled looks. It was past time to warn the police before something truly calamitous happened.

$$[\ 3 \ ]$$

"GERRY, I'm not sure you're listening," said Geneva. "These people are planning to storm the precinct on Saturday if you don't address this."

Lieutenant Gerry Nelson stood at the window, gazing wistfully out over the highway. It was a chilly Thursday morning, and a low fog had descended over the gravel and shrubs of the back parking lot. In the distance, they could hear the faint beeping of an eighteen-wheeler pulling into a grocery store.

"I'm not sure what you want me to do, Gen," he said at last. "These people have the right to peacefully assemble—"

"They have no intention of *peacefully* doing anything," Geneva replied. "You've met Hilda, so you know how...

intense she can be in her beliefs. Some people are drawn to that, I guess."

"Lost souls looking for meaning in their lives," said Gerry sadly. He tossed his disposable cup into a wastepaper basket. "If we start making arrests, they'll scatter like the disciples in Gethsemane."

Gerry had a total, and in Geneva's view, naïve confidence in the ability of the police force to weather any difficulty the locals could throw at them. "I should have recorded the rally they held on my lawn last night. I wish you could have felt the unity of that mob. It frightened me." She sank down into a chair in front of his desk. "All this fuss over a kidnapper. I just don't get it. If he'd murdered a woman, maybe—"

"Do you not remember when the case went to trial, ten or twelve years ago?" asked Gerry. "The media painted him in the darkest terms: 'The Wannabe Wife-Killer of Wrangler's Hill' and all that."

Geneva remembered the case being discussed, but only vaguely. "You can't expect me to recall something that happened that long ago. What did he do, exactly?"

"Well, that's the trouble," said Gerry, slapping his cap down on the desk. "Nobody really knows. He was notoriously tight-lipped at his own trial, and his wife—the one who was kidnapped—refused to cooperate with the prosecution for mysterious reasons. Based on what we've pieced together from eyewitnesses, they were driving down Highway 71 in the direction of Kroger... the car was swerving dangerously, and he was in the driver's seat, waving a gun at her. A single shot was fired, which struck the window on the front passenger's side."

"Where were they headed?" asked Geneva.

Gerry shrugged. "That's the extent of my knowledge. But it was enough for the jury to convict, based on the prosecutor's assertion that Mafelda was being transported against her will. If the bullet had struck her, we'd be facing an entirely different situation. He would never again have seen daylight."

"How does a marriage get to the point," said Geneva, "where one person is kidnapping and firing weapons at the other?"

"Marriage is hard," said Gerry. "Every relationship has those moments."

Geneva gave him an incredulous look. "You're not telling me you've ever wanted to murder—"

"I've been hit in the shoulder by a flying can of beans," said Gerry, smiling slightly. "Ivy swears it was an accident, but I had just made a very uncomplimentary remark about the dress she was wearing. 'You look like a walrus at a fancy dinner' or some such."

"I'd have hit you with a can of beans, too," said Geneva.

"Come to think of it," said Gerry, "so would I."

When Iris returned home that night, she was lugging a boxed set of five Agatha Christie novels she had bought at the used bookstore on Sterling Street. "Okay, so I've been writing this mystery novel for over two years and not making any progress." She flung the collection down on the kitchen table. "I figure it's time I studied the masters, and where better to start than with the Queen of Crime?"

"I'm surprised you didn't come to this conclusion years ago," said Geneva, who was slicing boiled eggs in preparation for making a salad. "When I went down to the station earlier—"

"You didn't seriously tell Gerry I've never read an Agatha Christie?" cried Iris, aghast. "Now the whole station is going to think I'm an idiot. 'There goes that lady who claims to be a detective and a mystery novelist but has not cracked open a single Christie novel.'"

"When you put it that way," said Geneva, "it does sound pretty bad."

Iris let out a resentful sigh and muttered dark imprecations under her breath.

"Anyway, I took a Lyft down to the station and spoke to Gerry"—Geneva tore open a package of dried cranberries and dumped them into a blue bowl—"and he says he read some of your early drafts of your novel—apparently you were emailing them to him?—"

"I did do that," said Iris, kicking off her shoes, "I don't know why."

"... and you're great at writing funny characters, but your problem is that you don't know how to properly structure a mystery. He said you're trying to write the story exactly as it happened to us in real life, but you're forgetting that real life isn't a novel and that what seemed exciting in real life might not work on the page."

Iris was silent for a moment. "He thinks my two heroines are *funny*? He thinks my book is *funny*?"

"Isn't that what you were going for?" said Geneva gingerly.

"*No*, it wasn't what I was going for." said Iris, her eyes burning holes in the vase in the center of the table. "It was supposed to be dark and *tragic* and melodramatic... he thinks Gwyneth and Irene are supposed to be *funny*?"

"I mean, objectively, aren't we kind of funny?" said Geneva quietly. "Anyway, which books did you get?"

Iris listed off the books—*Lord Edgware Dies, Three Act Tragedy, Peril at End House, The Murder at the Vicarage,* and *Toward Zero*—and was fuming over Agatha's infuriating ability to churn out masterpiece after masterpiece when Geneva's phone buzzed.

"That'll be George saying he needs picked up from work."

Lately, George had been jogging to work in the early mornings, but he often got stranded there on account of snow and had to be rescued.

But when she reached over and opened her texts, it wasn't George.

Hello, is this Geneva Pomolo? I've been following your career with interest for some time now. I don't know if you know me, but my name is Regina Baldwin, and I used to run marathons. I own a summer home at the edge of Wrangler's Hill.

Geneva read the text twice over, puzzled. She read it aloud to Iris, who dropped a can of ginger beer in surprise. "I thought Regina only spent her time in Sacramento."

"I know several people who used to work in entertainment," said Geneva, "who are now buying up land in the Midwest because the summers are too warm and crowded in California. Why do you think the Indiana film industry is suddenly thriving?"

"I figured it was just cheaper to film here, for tax reasons," said Iris, now on her hands and knees scrubbing up the amber liquid.

Geneva wasn't listening, though; Regina had just sent a follow-up text:

I'm supposed to be flying in tomorrow, but I came home a day early and I was wondering if you might like to meet up. There are some things that have happened in the past couple weeks that seriously worry me. I'm being threatened, I don't know by whom. I'm not trying to be melodramatic, but I think my life is in danger.

Geneva texted back at once: *Regina, hello. Have you gone to the police? I recommend going to the police first if you're being threatened.*

To which Regina replied, *Yes, but you know how seriously they take these things. Small-town precincts are under-manned and over-worked. I requested additional security for my gigs this weekend, and they refused. Said it was a waste of resources that could be better used elsewhere.*

Geneva thought back to the protest that Hilda had planned for Saturday, and to Gerry's assurance that the station wasn't in any danger. *Wrangler's PD is stretched thin this week,* she wrote back. *There's been some civil unrest.*

Where is that not the case, lately? Regina replied.

Geneva read the conversation back to Iris, who said, "Invite her over. Tell her we're almost finished making dinner, and she's welcome to it."

Geneva had a sudden wild vision of Regina Baldwin seated in the middle of their kitchen, eating a cranberry-and-boiled-egg salad. "Maybe we could meet her somewhere. She seems panicked, poor dear."

"Is my house not good enough?" asked Iris, gazing forlornly at the still-standing Christmas tree in the living room. Marvin, the corgi, came trotting down the stairs and into the kitchen, rolling over at Geneva's feet.

Geneva rubbed his soft white belly with one foot as she wrote, *How would you like to meet at our house for dinner in about an hour? My partner Iris will be here.*

To her surprise, Regina answered almost at once: *I can be there in thirty minutes. Are you sure you don't mind the imposition? What's your address?*

[4]

"I THINK someone is trying to poison me," said Regina. "Twice in the past month I've blacked out and woken several hours later, miles from where I started, with no recollection of how I got there. Chunks of my hair have been falling out, which is why I've taken to wearing a wig in public. I have constant stomach pain and back pain."

She was seated in the living room, a woman of about forty-five with blonde hair pinned up at the back, wearing a white woolen scarf and a black coat. In her right hand she clutched a mug of hot cocoa that Iris had prepared on the stove. George was kneeling in front of the hearth, trying to get a fire going, but he evidently was not having any success.

"These logs won't burn." he said in a pitiful tone. "I think they may have been left outside last night when it was snowing. When I went to the Home Depot—"

Geneva, who was in no mood for a long story, said, "Iris, would you help him with that?" To Regina she said, "Have you been to the doctor, though? What you're describing could just as soon be a... a sickness"—she didn't want to say *cancer*—"as a poisoning."

"Geneva—" said Regina, "do you mind if I call you Geneva? I have an uncanny intuition for this sort of thing. When I was sixteen, I remember telling my mother I had a terrible feeling about something. An hour later we got a call that my aunt Rhoda in Shreveport had died suddenly. She had lost her footing and fallen from a ladder."

"I don't mean to discredit your intuition," said Geneva gently, "but I've learned that in situations like this the simplest explanation is usually the correct one."

"I haven't fallen ill," Regina insisted. "I'm in the peak of health. And... and I simply can't go to a doctor with this. Not yet. My reputation as a health guru... I just can't."

Geneva studied her face with a twinge of sympathy. It must be difficult for her to acknowledge that she was getting older, and her body wasn't acting its best. Still, the woman was crazy for not going to a doctor.

"Do you have any reason to suspect someone might harbor a grudge against you?" Geneva asked.

"Besides the fact that I'm being slowly poisoned, you mean?" Regina laughed a mirthless laugh. "There have always been people who—let's just say, didn't like me. You can't grow up Jewish in this country without attracting a certain amount of hate. Back in August I came home to find that someone had spray-painted some truly horrific images on the door of my garage. They were straight out of the 1930s. That's been happening more and more often, the past three or four years."

"Worthless logs," mumbled Iris, who seemed to be having no better luck than George. "Stupid, idiotic logs."

Ignoring the outburst, Geneva said in a level tone, "Can you think of anyone in particular who might want to hurt you?"

Regina considered the question as she sipped her cocoa. "There was a girl in school who used to bully me—Blythe Bell, her name was. Her parents were divorced, and they didn't have a lot of money, and she took it out on me. I haven't seen her in about twenty years, but I don't think I've ever been hated so much by a single person."

Geneva jotted down the name in her notes app. "Who else?"

Regina hesitated. "There's a man who lives next to me... I almost feel bad saying this, because he's never been anything but kind outwardly..."

"What's his name?"

"Emmett," said Regina. "Emmett... Hickinbottom, I think. I always get this unpleasant feeling around him, like he secretly hates me and wants to hurt me in the most disturbing ways." She shook her head. "Again, I've learned to be careful. A man once asked me out on a date, and I turned him down, without having any particular reason for it. Years later I found out he had kidnapped his own wife. I have a gift, I think, for sizing people up at a glance."

"That would be so incredibly useful," said George, who had often gotten into trouble for trusting the wrong people.

"It has saved my neck on more than one occasion, I can tell you," said Regina, setting her mug down on the table. Marvin leapt up onto the sofa next to her, sniffing her curiously. "Anyway, a few weeks back, Emmett brought me coffee and a croissant from Starbucks—feeling a little guilty, I think—and ever since I drank the coffee, I've been experiencing all these weird symptoms. I think he may have put something in it."

"You started losing your hair right after drinking the coffee?" said Geneva.

"It took me three or four days to notice that something was really wrong. I'd been traveling for the past couple months—Florida, Maine, Wisconsin—and when I returned home to Wrangler's Hill at the end of November, that was when I started suffering health problems. I met Emmett on the morning of my first day back."

Geneva considered this for a moment in silence. Regina seemed bent on pinning her recent health woes on Emmett, but she wasn't convinced yet that there was a correlation. For one thing, it still wasn't clear that Emmett harbored any particular animus toward Regina. That could very well have all been in Regina's head.

"I've been doing some reading on antisemitism," said George, his face half-hidden behind three scarves. "It's terrifying."

"I'm afraid you can't know what it's really like," said Regina coolly, "unless you've experienced it personally."

"And you shared your concerns with the police?" said Geneva, eager not to get off-topic.

"Yes, but they're not taking me any more seriously than you have." There was a note of passive-aggression in her voice. "They told me I'm probably suffering some 'middle-aged women's ailment' and recommended seeing a doctor. I mean, imagine telling *me* that—it would be like offering Dr. Laura relationship advice."

"Yes, but in this case," said Geneva, "I don't see what it would hurt."

A frosty cordiality seemed to have settled over the room. Geneva couldn't convince Regina to pursue what she felt was the obvious solution, while Regina seemed to feel that no one was really listening to her. Politeness prevented both women from airing their obvious frustrations. Marvin, perhaps sensing the hostilities, glanced back and forth between them with a disconsolate expression.

"I'm really sorry," Geneva said at last. "I would love to help you, but until I see more proof that you're being poisoned—"

"I'm suffering the effects of prolonged poisoning," said Regina. "I googled them."

"The internet isn't always the most reliable source for medical information. I'm not saying this is all in your head, you're obviously suffering some affliction, but I question whether a crime is being committed. If a crime isn't being committed, then this is really out of my purview."

Later Geneva would have good reason to regret having spoken so sharply. In the moment, however, George and Iris nodded agreement.

"I think..." said Iris slowly. "I think an exam might be able to tell us *what's* poisoning you, if anything. At the bookstore I saw a book on the use of poison as a murder weapon in Agatha Christie's novels. Perhaps I could read it and give you a diagnosis."

"I don't think a book about a series of fictional mysteries is going to help me," said Regina, rising and reaching for her keys, "though by all means—"

"Agatha worked in a hospital during the war," said George knowledgeably. "She knew all about poisons."

Regina was talking over him as though he hadn't spoken. "Apologies for taking up so much of your evening. I'll just say this, for most of my life there have been people—usually just one or two at a time—who have hated me and done everything in their power to torment me. They did it in such a way that hardly anyone noticed. And when I tried to tell others, I was mocked, belittled, laughed at. 'You're imagining things, Regina.' 'Surely it can't be as bad as all that.'"

She strode across the room to the door, where she turned round. "And I thought maybe when I grew up, when I started racking up achievements in sports and business, finally, finally. maybe they would listen. But they've never listened. And they're not listening still."

"Regina, really—" cried Geneva, but it was no use. Regina had already opened the door and stalked out, leaving a tense and chilly silence behind her.

[5]

WHEN GENEVA AWOKE on Saturday morning, she found several cars parked in Hilda's driveway and at the side of the street, would-be protesters eagerly spilling out onto the lawn as they waited for her to emerge from the house.

"Wouldn't it have made more sense," said Iris over a light breakfast of toast and egg whites, "for them to simply meet at the station? Why go through all the trouble of meeting here and then carpooling?"

"I think Hilda wants to go over protocol before they head out there." Geneva sprinkled some salt over her eggs. "What to do in case of arrest, that sort of thing."

"I think the easiest way to avoid arrest would be to just go home," said Iris. "Make some French toast, put on a little music…"

"Legally they have the right to protest as long as they maintain a certain distance. Gerry said he's prepared to make arrests if he must, but he hopes it won't come to that."

"Let's hope."

Geneva scraped the last of the jam over her toast. "I've been thinking about what Regina said the other night—about how she once nearly dated a man who then kidnapped his own wife. Do you think…?"

"No way," said Iris, patting down her hair. Her curls were unusually springy this morning. "Mordecai Whistler can't be the only man in the Midwest ever to have engaged in wife-napping. If it was him, that's a remarkable coincidence."

"Is it a coincidence, though?" said Geneva, unscrewing the lid of a bottled water. "When was Mordecai released from prison?"

Iris did a quick search on her phone. "It says he's been out for a couple weeks. Some relatives set up a legal fund—they seem to think he was wrongly imprisoned— and he managed to raise over a hundred thousand dollars. Oh, and…" She raised one brow. "Apparently some friends and supporters are planning a counter-protest this morning."

Geneva set down her fork. Two different groups converging on the station, one wholly convinced of his innocence, the other wanting him driven out of the community. "I truly hope Gerry is ready," she said quietly.

"Are *we* ready?" Iris replied and rose to rinse her plate.

———

The race was beginning at Camp Round-About, along the banks of the White River in northwest Wrangler's Hill. Geneva and Iris arrived at around 11:30 that morning, where they found numerous food trucks and aid stations set up at the gates of the camp. Dozens of people of all ages were pacing about stamping their feet and trying to keep warm. A long row of port-a-potties stood against the trees like a barricade. Regina Baldwin, bundled up tightly against the cold in a woolly coat, was speaking in low tones to a tiny old woman whose face was wrinkled like an old gown.

"No, I'm not feeling well, Aunt Clara," Geneva heard her say. "But when has that ever stopped me?"

"I almost feel bad for nudging you into hosting this marathon," said the woman named Clara. "You ought to be sitting at home by the fire, eating soup and getting over this mysterious illness."

"Oh, I don't mind," said Regina, dismissing her concerns with a wave of her hand. "It's brought a ton of good press to Wrangler's Hill, and that means more money for the community. Maybe they'll expand the library."

"Wouldn't that be nice," said Aunt Clara, absently pulling out a tissue and wiping her runny nose.

A few paces away, meanwhile, stood a man in a black suit and black hat, with a gold chain around his neck, his arms spread wide like a saint ascending into heaven. As he ranted, a small crowd began to gather with an air of mild interest.

"There is a darkness in this town," he was saying. "The great beast, Leviathan, stalks our streets. In the stacks of the public library, I found a three-hundred-year-old diary written by one of the first women to settle in Wrangler's Hill, in which she describes how the townsmen were hunted by a monstrous creature who emerged from the lake and offered them the deepest desires of their hearts. She calls him 'the Tempter, the Wicked One.' Friends, he is still with us."

A silence followed in which the only sound was the wind banging the doors of the port-a-potties. No one quite knew what to do with the news that their town was haunted by a monster.

"I'm Christabel Dollar," he went on, "and I came here three years ago hoping to hunt the beast to his lair—"

"Christabel, are you bothering these people again?" came a voice at his elbow, and a young man in a black cap, with a ginger beard, came striding over. "Regina was very clear that she wanted no *grifters* at this event."

"Emmett, I have nothing to sell," said Christabel, looking peeved by the interruption. "But I've been in dozens of houses, and I've seen the worst this town has to offer. In the suburbs of Pike's Moth, I was nearly strangled by an invisible serpent, seven feet long—"

"Ignore him, folks," Emmett said to the assembled crowd. "The first exorcism is free, but the second... the second will cost you."

Emmett smirked to himself and walked on—along with most of the crowd, who began to disperse, having apparently sized up the exorcist and decided Emmett was right.

Geneva followed him with her eyes as he strode over to a garishly painted taco truck and bought a large breakfast taco stuffed with bacon and avocado. "Regina knew an Emmett," she said in a low voice. "Do you think—"

"Here's an idea," said Iris, "if he tries to hand her a coffee, we *run* over there and knock it out of her hands before she can take a sip."

"I'm not sure she would take it, in any case," said Geneva. "She seems terrified of him."

"What if something were to happen today, though? The police already seem to have their hands full, and they've obviously ignored Regina's request for additional security."

Geneva had been wondering this herself. Every policeman in Wrangler's was currently at the station, helping to defend it from the protesters. If a fight broke out, or Christabel needed to be escorted from the premises, or, heaven forbid, someone leapt out of the crowd and tried to attack Regina, who would be able to prevent it?

"Well, we have Hilda to thank for that," said Geneva miserably. "Every time she tries to help out, she ends up causing chaos."

Regina had been conspicuously avoiding the two women ever since their arrival. At present she was standing beneath a bare oak taking slow sips from a water bottle and clutching her side with a pained look. With a feeling of growing concern, Geneva began crossing the broad commons and Iris followed; but before they could reach her, a woman in a black turtleneck and black jeans came running up, waving a phone in one hand. It was Serenity Sparklan, the obnoxious freelance journalist who had once assisted Geneva in investigating a murder.

"My mother just texted me and asked if I had seen what's going down at the police department," said Serenity loudly. "I pulled it up on the WRNG news website."

A small crowd began to cluster around her, Geneva and Iris among them. A video was streaming live from outside the station, where a mob of between fifty to seventy-five people was swarming the parking lot, darkly chanting "NO MORE CONVICTS IN OUR TOWN."

A young man in a red beanie and a denim jacket embroidered with the American flag had leapt onto a police car, and was taking a savage glee in jumping up and down on the roof. After a minute or two, the glass of the windshield began to splinter and crack. Through the windows of the station Geneva could see a couple of officers looking on ineffectually as if confused.

There was no sign of Hilda, although the crowd was big enough by now that it might have swallowed her.

"For those of you who are just tuning in," came the voice of Helga Keyshanks, a local reporter, "I'm standing outside the Wrangler's Hill Police Department, where a crowd has gathered demanding the re-imprisonment of recently released felon Mordecai Whistler. Lieutenant Gerry Nelson, barricaded within the precinct, has just issued a statement saying, quote: 'No one here has the power to put a man back in prison, and we will never surrender to the craven forces of mob justice.'"

"Bless him," cried Geneva. "We have a brave soul."

"Gen, he could be killed," said Iris. "They're outnumbered in there by about thirty to one."

Geneva couldn't imagine that the mob would actually storm the station, but they seemed restless and agitated, and Gerry's statement had done nothing to quell their fury. She saw now that several of the people gathered near the front of the building held stones or bricks in their upraised hands. One went flying and landed in a shrub near the ruined car. It was followed soon after by a second, which hit its target—smashing through the window where Lieutenant Sheehan had been standing just moments before, spraying glass all over the snow-speckled lawn.

"I truly hope they've radioed for help," said Iris, but the crowd seemed undeterred by the prospect of mass arrests. Already the most foolhardy among them were descending on the open window, while the beleaguered policemen attempted to block the entrance with a filing cabinet pulled from some back office.

"That's not going to keep those people out," said Emmett, who had been watching the chaos from over Geneva's shoulder. "They're out for blood."

"No, but it might buy them some time," said Iris. "This is playing on all the local news channels; within a few minutes, that parking lot will be swarming with cops."

"A couple of friends actually tried to recruit me into joining the protest." Emmett shook his head in disgust. "There's no way I'd be a party to something like that. Destroying a police station is a serious crime, and everyone who participates in this mess is likely to be arrested."

"This is the hour of darkness," came a voice at his elbow. They turned to see Christabel, looking newly resplendent in a white rhinestone suit. "Local witches are behind this, mark my words."

"Did... did you just change clothes?" Iris asked in surprise.

"Christabel, with all due respect," said Emmett, "what we're seeing is the result of complicated political and social forces." He motioned to the tiny screen, where the police were now beating back invading protesters with riot shields. "You're not going to reverse all of that by finding an old drawing of a monster in the library, or whatever."

"That's the kind of skepticism that keeps this town in chains," said Christabel, with theatrical indignation.

Serenity Sparklan, who had been holding the phone all this while, motioned for silence.

"It's hard to tell just what's going on," said Helga, "in the chaos behind me... someone appears to have set off a smoke bomb on the lawn, or is that... I'm sorry, I'm being told that's just fog..."

"Honestly, how did this woman ever get on TV?" said Serenity.

"... and now some of the counter-protesters are placing them-selves between the rioters and the station... they're literally shielding the police with their own bodies... one of the protesters takes a swing at a young woman in a Dodgers ball cap... the swing misses her by inches... she's come prepared and now she's spraying him with pepper spray..."

"Iris, that's Natalie," said Geneva.

"Natalie who?"

"Your niece, Natalie!"

Iris stared at the phone in disbelief. Natalie's thin frame and flaming red hair were unmistakable. "Good girl," she said.

It was nearing twelve, and they had been watching the livestream for nearly ten minutes. Serenity pulled the phone away somewhat abruptly. "I really shouldn't be here," she said. "I should be down there interviewing anyone involved who will talk to me... I have a feeling the *Bugle* would pay handsomely for first-hand reporting from someone who was there on the scene."

"I thought the *Bugle* was no longer taking your calls," Iris pointed out.

"Nothing is ever permanent in journalism," said Serenity, and with a final apologetic smile, she trotted off.

A gust of wind blew across the commons, ripping a pennant from a little girl's hand. It made loops in the air and landed about forty feet away in a muddy puddle of thawing snow. At the gates, the runners were getting into position, doing last-minute stretches and lunges in their running tights and loose-fitting, long-sleeved shirts. A few of them seemed to be regretting having agreed to a marathon on such an unwelcoming day. Geneva scanned the grounds for Regina and found her seated atop an overturned yellow bucket at the foot of a tree, hands on her stomach, her face aflame. Incredibly, she appeared to be sweating.

Alarmed, Geneva went running over to her and Iris followed.

"I'll be fine, I think," said Regina in a tone of grim determination. "I just need to get through the next five or six hours, and then I can go home."

"Regina, you don't look well," said Geneva, resisting the urge to place a motherly hand on her face. "If you're sick—I mean really sick, and you certainly look it—nobody's going to force you to host this."

Regina shrugged away the suggestion. "A Baldwin always keeps her commitments," she said, and attempted to stand but immediately sank back down again. "I just need to..."

She trailed off.

"Gen, she's getting delirious," said Iris. "One of us needs to call an ambulance."

"Don't they usually have doctors on-site during marathons?" said Geneva. "Seems like a pretty egregious omission to over-look that."

Iris retrieved her phone and dialed 9-1-1. She explained the situation and gave the dispatcher their location. "You really couldn't have picked a worse time," said the dispatcher, whose name was Shirley. "Both of our medical teams are currently down at the precinct tending to riot victims."

"How long will it take to get someone here?" asked Iris, with an anxious glance at her partner.

"I want to say, maybe an hour or two, but I can't make any promises. If your friend's in really bad shape, your best bet is to get her in a car and drive her down yourself."

"We'll be there in a few minutes." She hung up the phone.

Geneva placed a hand on Regina's shoulders and attempted to coax her into getting up. By now Regina was so insensible that she seemed barely aware of their presence. "Walk with us to the car, dear... it's just over here at the foot of the hill. We're going to have you looked at, if that's all right."

"And even if it's not," said Iris, "you're getting in the car."

Regina said nothing by way of resistance. Instead, she stood for a moment looking disoriented, like a woman standing on the edge of a bridge about to jump off. Then, with a worrying swiftness, she sank down into the snow and lay perfectly still.

Geneva circled around her for a moment, feeling the first stirrings of panic.

"We'll need to carry her the rest of the way," she said. "Or get someone else to carry her."

But Iris, who was already kneeling beside her, merely shook her head. "I'm afraid it may already be too late for that. She's not breathing; she doesn't have a pulse. Gen, I... I think she might be dead."

[6]

Geneva stood silent for a moment, wishing she could shut her eyes and undo the scene that confronted her. The marathon that was scheduled to begin in six minutes would likely have to be cancelled. Given the riots at the station, it could be hours before the police arrived. And there was something else—a nagging guilt that she should have listened to Regina more closely when Regina had warned her...

Then again, if Regina had gone to a doctor...

Geneva only allowed herself a moment's reflection, however, before directing her focus to the tasks at hand.

By now the news that Regina had collapsed was beginning to circulate through the grounds, but few had yet guessed she was dead. Waving Emmett over, she said to him quietly, "I need you to get on the megaphone and let everyone know that this event has been cancelled."

"Do you have the authority to make that decision?" asked Emmett.

"I'm making it," said Geneva. "A woman is dead."

Emmett gazed at her in disbelief, then turned to look back at the body of the woman lying beneath the tree.

As he ran for the megaphone, Geneva strode over to Iris, who was still kneeling over the body. She looked as though she harbored a faint hope that it might suddenly sit up and begin breathing again. "I think it's fair to say," said Iris, "that she was not in the best of health."

"She knew that. It's baffling to me that she refused to do anything about it."

"Too much professional pride, I imagine." Iris gazed mournfully down at the prostrate figure. "If you've spent your life being told you're a health expert, why would you need to see a professional?"

Geneva thought back to what Regina had said in their living room two nights before, about a bigotry that had dogged her during her entire life. "Maybe it's time to reconsider what she was trying to tell us. She seemed to think she was being targeted because of her race."

Iris gazed probingly at her partner. "Really? She didn't seem to have any evidence, aside from a vague feeling."

"Given that she's dead now, I'd say the feeling is due for reassessment."

Iris nodded, as if to concede the point. "I'd like to know what Giles thinks—whether she was poisoned or died of natural causes." Giles was a clinical pathologist who assisted the local police.

"I'll call him," said Geneva, standing to her feet. "Surely he's not trapped in the station—what's going on down there, by the way?"

"I haven't been following the news," said Iris, "I got distracted."

She brought up the livestream on her phone. Someone had released canisters of tear gas on the lawn outside the station, and the gas mingled with the fog to create a pearlescent veil cloaking the station from view. A woman knelt on the sidewalk in front of a parking meter, rubbing her tear-stained eyes ineffectually.

"I can't imagine our local department having canisters of tear gas just lying around," said Geneva. "The cavalry must have arrived."

Emmett, meanwhile, had informed the dismayed crowd that the marathon had been cancelled "owing to an event beyond anyone's control." There followed an outpouring of panicked questions, as people demanded to know what had become of Regina—whose body was plainly visible a few yards behind him—and whether an ambulance had been called. Given her stature and celebrity, the news of her death was going to be a nasty shock.

Geneva walked off a little way by herself, staying close to the roadside, until the entrance to the camp had receded into the distance. She made three attempts to call Giles. He answered on the third call, sounding grumpy—apparently, he had been ice-fishing on Lake Alpaca with his twelve-year-old son—but agreed to drive over at once when he learned of Regina's death.

"That poor woman," he said softly. "Around here she's as beloved as Oprah. Who'd want to harm her?"

"We don't know that she was murdered yet," said Geneva.

"No. But in this town…"

He left the sentence unfinished. Geneva let him go and trudged back up the snowy hill toward the campground, where she found the assembly in varying degrees of shock and disbelief.

"I should have seen this coming," said Freya, jangling her colorful bracelets. "Someone in the neighborhood social media group last week was saying they think there's something in the water, that we're being slowly poisoned—that the globalists are inserting chemicals to make us more obedient and complacent, like sheep."

"That's utter rubbish," said Emmett, sounding deeply offended. "If the water was being poisoned, why is only one of us dead?"

"But she's not the only one," said Freya gravely. "Remember the chef who died at Christmas, what was his name—"

Geneva couldn't resist intervening. "Chester wasn't killed by the tap water; he was done in by a deranged person on a quest for revenge."

"But don't you see, that proves it," said Freya, gazing solemnly round. "One by one, they're going to kill us all."

Emmett flexed his hands as if wanting to hit something. Geneva's eyes fell on a middle-aged man in a garish pink tracksuit, dark hair impeccably coiffed, who was gazing serenely down at the body from behind enormous old-fashioned aviators.

Sensing that he was being watched, the man said, "But then, who could blame someone for wanting to kill her? She, who caused so much disappointment and anguish—"

Geneva blinked back surprise; even murderers usually waited until the body was cold before airing their beefs with the dead. "What disappointments?"

"I'm sure I don't need to tell you." He coughed, once, into a lace handkerchief. "She had a reputation in Wrangler's Hill for being fickle and unreliable. She broke every contract, stiffed every partner, reneged on every promise—"

"I'm sorry, did you *date* her?" asked Iris, in a tone of mild surprise.

The man in the pink tracksuit laughed politely. "No, and I never would have—her first two marriages failed, you know—"

"That doesn't tell us a thing about *her*," Iris pointed out. "People get divorced for loads of reasons."

Perhaps sensing he was outnumbered, the man glanced shiftily back and forth between the two women and suddenly faded back into the crowd. "I'd like to have gotten his name," said Geneva. "He obviously knew something he wasn't sharing."

"Just wanted attention, I expect," said Iris. "People always want to pretend they know a celebrity more than they do."

Geneva wasn't wholly convinced, though. Even if he hadn't personally known her, he had certainly heard things. "*She had a reputation in Wrangler's Hill..."* Where had he learned that?

"She bought a breakfast taco from the taco stand, shortly before she started complaining of stomach pains. I'd like to speak to the person running that truck. Also, she mentioned that her home had been vandalized last August—I wonder if the police ever followed up on that, if a report was filed, if the culprit was ever apprehended."

"We may have to take a trip down to her house," said Iris. "It's in the ritzier part of town—I don't go there much."

"We'll speak to her neighbors and see if they witnessed anything. There may even be CCTV footage... if we can get hold of it, we might be able to pinpoint whomever has been harassing her."

Iris didn't look too sure. "If the police weren't able to find them—"

"I don't think the police looked particularly hard."

Already the crowd was beginning to disperse, having accepted that they weren't going to witness any sporting events. Christabel Dollar stood at the crest of a hill, arms spread wide, ranting rather ghoulishly about a "specter of death" haunting the community. No one much seemed to be listening. A young woman with faded freckles, blonde hair falling over her face in ringlets, glanced darkly through the front-facing window of the taco truck as she emptied the till. Freya and Emmett were standing together, talking.

"I'd like to move south, I think," she was saying. "Houston or New Orleans, somewhere warm. I don't like living in the Midwest, especially not in the winter months. The grief is still fresh."

"What could you possibly have to grieve for?" asked Emmett, more out of politeness than interest. "You always seem to be living in a world of your own, untouched by tragedy."

"You'd be surprised," said Freya. "On Christmas Eve seven years ago, my fiancé left me."

"Did he give a reason?"

Freya gaze him a puzzled look. "Reason?"

"For breaking up with you."

"We didn't break up," said Freya. "He died."

And without another word she turned and began trudging down the hill to her van.

[7]

As GENEVA WAS LEAVING church on the following day, she found that Giles had messaged her. *Finished examining the body,* he wrote, *and I think we can safely rule out the normal ravages of aging. She was poisoned—by arsenic, primarily, although copper and lead were also present. If you're thinking someone spiked her coffee, as Ms. Reeves suggested yesterday, I'd like to hear how you explain the lead and copper.*

Geneva texted back (accidentally jostling an old lady pushing a pram in the process): *Is there no way of knowing how the poison entered her system?*

I'm afraid not. One thing I can tell you, though: this had been going on for some time. Whoever did it was doing it slowly and methodically over many weeks. In small quantities it wouldn't

have been lethal or detectable—she would have felt only vague
pains—but then at some point, well...

The conversation with Giles struck something in Geneva's
memory, and she spent much of the afternoon trying to
remember just what. Only late in the afternoon when Iris
came gliding into the living room with Geneva's own battered
copy of *The Mysterious Affair at Styles* pressed to her nose,
did she feel a twinge of recognition. "Hang on... how far have
you gotten in that?"

"Only about midway," said Iris. "I figured I may as well read
them in chronological order, and this was her first book."

"She had some real clunkers in her twenties," said Geneva. "I
only ask because I have a vague memory of how that one
ends... can I see it for a moment?"

Reluctantly Iris handed over the book. Geneva flipped to the
end and spent a few minutes reading. "Yes, just as I thought...
the story hinges on—"

"Wait, are you really about to spoil the ending?" said Iris
loudly.

"Well, you'll see what I mean when you get there. Suffice to
say it involves the victim being slowly poisoned over a period
of weeks." Geneva tapped her nose absently. "Now you've
got me thinking—"

"You think maybe we're dealing with a literate murderer? Someone who's ripping off the killings in Agatha Christie?"

"I mean, her murders are ingenious," said Geneva. "If I was a killer... but no, at this point, we have no reason to think it's anything more than coincidence. I'd like to know the mechanism by which the poisons were administered—how do you inadvertently imbibe copper and lead over a period of weeks without knowing...?"

She was talking half to herself now, and Iris, who had stolen the book back, was only half-listening. Before church that morning Geneva had sent an email to Gerry recounting the events of the aborted marathon and asking if he knew the name of the man in the pink track suit.

However, Gerry was busy filling out paperwork—half the rioters had been arrested the day before and the other half had dispersed, "leaving twenty-three people who need to be processed into the system," he told her. "Funnily enough, even though your friend Hilda seems to have been the chief instigator, she melted away at the first sign of trouble—we haven't been able to locate her on video."

None of this answered her question, so Geneva had sent a follow-up email gently asking about the man in the track suit. "No, but judging from what he told you, it sounds like Regina might have gotten him into some kind of legal trouble. Might be worth following up on. Post a notice on Facebook and see if anyone bites."

Geneva did just that. When she and Iris went out later that night to meet some friends for coffee and poker at the Steamy Bean, she asked Iris to drive slowly "just in case we happen to see him. If he's still wearing yesterday's get-up, he won't be hard to miss."

Iris was still recovering from a recent cold, one that had kept her largely insensible during their last investigation at Christmas, and the floorboard of the back seat was piled high with empty tissue boxes. "I promise I'll get this cleaned out as soon as things settle down a little. Valentine's Day is coming up, and I don't want to scare away any prospective partners with a filthy station wagon."

"Iris, I'm not worried about the clutter," said Geneva, gazing through the window at the twilit streets. "If we end up having to make a citizen's arrest, then yes, we'll need the space back there—"

"Can we do that?" asked Iris brightly. "Is this another crime thing I don't know about because I haven't read Agatha Christie?"

She parked the car at the back of the Steamy Bean and the two women filed into the shop. The sole topic of conversation during the poker game, as it had been all over Wrangler's Hill since the previous day, was the apparent murder of Regina Baldwin. It had even crowded out the attempted storming of the precinct as the major story on all the local news programs and morning talk shows.

"I'm barely old enough to remember the Kennedy assassination," said Heather Grahame, a graying woman with bright eyes in a pink coat and pink scarf, "but I remember my mother telling me how upsetting it was, realizing that someone so powerful could die like that. That's sort of how I feel now. Regina was like a *queen*."

"Seems awfully cowardly, slowly poisoning someone like that," said Millicent Burrows, a woman of forty or forty-five who worked at one of the county libraries, and wore a jaunty sweater. "If I wanted to kill someone, I'd look them straight in the face and pull the trigger. I'd want them to know I had done it."

"You're braver than me," said Heather, taking her mug of cocoa in both hands. "Death is so messy and horrible. I don't think I could bring myself to do that to another human being. Even if I hated them more than anyone living."

"Oh, I think anyone could be driven to do it under the right circumstances," said Geneva, clicking her poker chips together absently. "I've known too many sweet, pious old ladies who suddenly found themselves needing to get rid of an inconvenient husband, or wanting revenge on a girl from their school days for whom they'd been harboring a grudge since they were sixteen…"

Millicent's eyes brightened at the mention of revenge. "I knew Regina when we were very young," she said. "We went to school together, and knowing her, you wouldn't have thought she'd grow up to be someone that people looked up to."

She seemed to glow as she spoke; it was clear she had been waiting to say this for much of the conversation. There was a faint stirring of anticipation. "Mill, you can't just leave us hanging like that," said Iris. "I remember reading somewhere that the great always have a sense of their own greatness, even as children. Surely there must have been some indication, even then—"

"Not even a little," said Millicent, smiling slightly. "She was short for her age and sort of chubby—I think half her fixation on health and fitness came from being picked on in school. Girls can be really savage, especially in high school, before we've been kicked around by the world and learned a little humility. I remember one girl, Belle—"

She paused for a long while, as if summoning some half-forgotten recollection.

"No, it was Blythe," she said finally. "*Bell* was her last name. I wonder whatever became of her, if she ever sees Regina on television and thinks, 'Look at that idiot—she made it and I didn't.'"

"Not a fan of Regina's, I take it," Geneva prompted.

"That's a bit of an understatement," said Millicent. "They *hated* each other. Granted, Regina had good reason for hating Blythe. She was always bullying her for being fat, and bookish, and for her religion—the Baldwins were devoutly Jewish, and everyone knew it. And Regina was a brilliant student, beloved of every teacher, president of the honor society and so on, and I think that may have bred a certain resentment. There was something about her that just drove Blythe *mad.*"

"How did she bully her?" asked Iris, who had been bullied herself as a girl and took a keen interest in the subject.

"There was an... incident," said Millicent slowly, gazing into her mug. "The police were called. Blythe was nearly expelled from school. Her dad was a powerful lawyer, and he managed to calm the waters, assuring the school board that it wouldn't happen again. Not that it mattered by then—Blythe had made herself socially radioactive. No decent person wanted to associate with her. She'd hoped to ostracize Regina and ended up being ostracized herself."

This was promising. If Blythe still lived anywhere in the vicinity, or had visited recently, she would move to the top of their suspect list.

"Whatever became of her?" Geneva asked.

"You know, I saw her at the grocers' five or six months ago. You know how they say some people age quicker than others —middle age hit her *hard*. She had dark rings around her eyes, as if someone had struck her in the face. Her nails were yellow, and her skin had that wrinkly texture peculiar to smokers. She was missing a couple teeth." Millicent smiled. "Look, I won't pretend I'm a saint. We were passing a rack of magazines and Regina happened to be gracing that week's cover of *Health & Fitness*. Right as she walked past, I pointed at the magazine and said, 'Bet you wish that was you, huh?'"

The table let out a collective gasp. "You didn't," said Iris.

Millicent nodded. "But of course, I regretted it a moment later, because instead of getting angry she just gave me the saddest look. I don't think I've ever seen that expression on another living creature. To the end of my days, I pray I never have to see it again."

Geneva ordered the table another round of drinks and they went on with their game.

The store closed at nine. As they returned to the station wagon, Geneva said, "Five or six months ago... Regina mentioned that someone had vandalized her summer home back in August."

"Do you think—"

"Do I think maybe Millicent's crack at the supermarket goaded her into rekindling an old quarrel? No idea." Geneva buckled her seatbelt with a snap. "But I think it's time we found her. At the very least, she could tell us what she did that was so horrible all those years ago."

Iris spent a few minutes letting the car warm up and then backed out of the parking lot. They rode together in silence as she approached an intersection at the top of a high hill. The road sloped below them, and the lights of the strip mall glittered like a box of old jewels.

The engine rattled ominously, like a child playing with castanets. "Come on, don't die on me," said Iris. "This car's been giving me trouble for about a week now."

"You've had it for about fifteen years," Geneva pointed out. "Might be time to think about getting a new one."

"Absolutely not," said Iris, but at that moment, there came a terrible ticking from the engine and the car sputtered and died.

Iris let out an oath. She turned the key once in the ignition, but the car wheezed and groaned and fell silent.

"Well, at least there's no one behind us," said Geneva. "I can call George and have him drive out and come get us."

"I'm more worried about the panhandlers. We're in the part of town where they tend to congregate." She pressed a button on her remote key and all the doors locked. "Don't look now, but I think there's one heading toward us."

"I've got some cash in my purse," said Geneva, reaching into the floorboard. Iris threw her a reproachful glance. "If they're panhandling at this time of year, in this weather, they must really need it. I just wish I had more to give them."

"You're a better person than me," Iris said low—then flinched in alarm, for someone was now tapping at her window.

Geneva looked over, preparing to hand him the money—then let out a cry of surprise. At the door of the car stood a middle-aged man, dark hair slicked back like Elvis, wearing a pair of dark aviators and a garish pink tracksuit.

"IRIS, IT'S HIM. It's *him*," she exclaimed, pointing a crooked finger at the window in warning.

"Him who?" cried Iris, aghast.

"The man from the marathon."

"There were about three hundred people at the marathon."

"The one we've been looking for, you goober."

He seemed to have recognized them, too, for at the sight of Geneva he seized up in surprise and began a dangerous-looking sprint down the ice-covered hill. He had sprinted at least fifty yards and was getting further and further away with each moment they sat arguing. His legs wobbled unsteadily, as if at any moment they might give way beneath him.

"Iris, start the car—*start the car*," Geneva cried.

"Give me a minute." Iris turned the key once more in the ignition, but the car remained resolute and motionless.

Geneva shut her eyes for a moment and drew a deep breath. When she opened them again, the man was still in sight but rapidly fading from view. "The only way we're going to catch him at this point is if we go running after him."

"He's in his forties and we're both pushing sixty," Iris pointed out. "If you want a titanium hip, that's how you get it."

"No, we'd never catch him running." She sat for a moment, thinking. "I remember reading an Agatha Christie where a guy put on a pair of skis to get across a village in ten minutes and commit a murder—"

"Does your brain always go back to Agatha Christie?" asked Iris, chuckling.

"Yours would, too, if you had read her. Anyway, you wouldn't happen to have a pair of skis back there, would you?"

"No, I haven't been skiing since before the murder of Horace what's-his-name—"

"Weatherspoon," said Geneva, who had a good memory for these things. "Did George maybe leave his skis back there?"

Iris turned round in her seat, surveying the mess in the back. "Doesn't look like it... there's nothing that would help us, just piles and piles of empty Kleenex boxes."

"Those will have to do, then," said Geneva in a tone of resolve. "Would you hand me a couple?"

"What, why?"

"Never mind why, just do it." Just up the street, near the bottom of the hill, the man in the pink tracksuit was jogging past Creswell's Countertops Fabricators.

Warily Iris reached back and handed one of the boxes to her partner, who was already unlacing and pulling off her boots. "Gen, I've seen you do some weird things, and I never stopped you—"

"Two please," said Geneva, "I need two boxes."

With a shrug Iris reached back and handed her a second box. "You do realize that no one is making you do this?"

"We can worry about that later," said Geneva, wriggling her left foot into one of the boxes. "Call George and tell him to meet us in front of the countertop store—I'll see you in like six minutes."

"If you really think I'm following you—." cried Iris, but Geneva was already climbing out of the car, both feet clad in tissue boxes.

She wasn't sure it would work at first—perhaps the ice wasn't slick enough—but she needn't have worried, for the second she dropped down onto the street she nearly slipped and fell. Quickly grabbing hold of the passenger's side mirror, she eased herself slowly toward the front of the car. All of Wrangler's Hill lay before her, and she had only to let go and go flying forward into the cold, against the night wind, praying she was still alive when she reached the foot of the hill.

[8]

THE SECONDS that followed were some of the more terrifying of her life. Geneva had no control over where she was headed; she was descending an icy hill at a speed that could prove crippling if she slammed into a streetlamp or fell and landed face-first on the sidewalk. It reminded her of the roller coaster she had ridden at the summer carnival a few years before, the way her breath seemed to leave her lungs as if she had been punched in the chest. Odd spots danced at the edges of her eyes; she felt as though she was going to throw up every bite of the salad she'd had for dinner...

Seeing a blur of pink to her left, she reached for it... she and the blur went tumbling into a heap on the sidewalk in a flurry of muffled oaths. The blur of pink had broken her fall; she was alive and unharmed... she allowed herself a moment's rest before getting back up, savoring the exhilaration of being able to breathe again.

"Will... you... get... off?" cried the pink bundle. He had lost his aviators and was now half-heartedly trying to shove Geneva aside so that he could find them. "What are you thinking, attacking a man like that? And what's that on your feet? Coming down the street like that, you could've been killed."

"Why did you run?" demanded Geneva, slowly recovering her ability to speak.

"What do you mean, why did I run? You were both shrieking. I could see you were about to come after me."

"A man doesn't run unless he has something to hide," said Geneva, feeling a stab in her backside. She had fallen on the aviators and broken them. "What were you running from?"

The man sputtered an indignant response. At the same instant, Iris came clopping toward them in her knee-high boots, panting and out of breath.

"I just spoke to George," she said. "Tow truck's on its way. *He's* on his way."

"This is an ambush," said the man, "an assault. I could have you both arrested."

"Good luck with that," said Geneva. "The police have their hands full at the moment."

"Listen, I'd love to sit out here and fight all night," said Iris, hunched over with her hands on her legs, "but can we take it somewhere warmer? I just tried to spit, and the spit froze in midair."

———

They found a wine and spirits store that was still open, and they crowded into a dimly lit corner where there was less chance of being overheard. Once a minute or so, the manager would glance back to make sure they weren't bundling liquor into their coats, so the two women pretended to be shopping and encouraged the man in the pink tracksuit to do the same.

"Listen, I'm only cooperating in the hopes that maybe it'll get you off my back," said the man, whose name was Clyde. "You've got about ten minutes before I walk out that door, and if you try to stop me, I'll tell the manager I'm being held against my will."

Not the most promising of beginnings, but Geneva wasn't going to waste precious time arguing. "If I were you, I'd want to stay indoors as long as possible. Why the rush?"

"I'm not *homeless*. I just... well, I just needed some extra cash." Clyde brushed a hand against a bottle of Blanc de

Blanc. "Granted, this isn't exactly what I pictured myself doing at forty-five."

"I can't imagine panhandling pays the bills."

"It's not my *only* source of income," said Clyde.

Iris, who had been eyeing a bottle of bubbly with a longing expression, turned him a searching look. "I hope your second source of income pays better."

"It used to."

"We've got about eight minutes," said Geneva, who had been keeping an eye on the clock, "so you'll need to be a little less vague."

"I don't really want to get into it. Suffice to say, I was recently stiffed by a major client and lost what would have been the biggest endorsement of the year. We're talking Dolly Parton-level endorsement."

Geneva looked at him shrewdly. "Would this client happen to have been recently murdered?"

The silence that followed this question seemed to suggest yes.

"Did the endorsement fall through *because* she was murdered?" asked Iris.

Clyde winced at the question. "No. I've been dealing with the fallout from this for weeks and weeks. I'm a fashion designer by trade, or I was. An old girlfriend from Biloxi happened to meet Regina's agent at a cocktail party and put her in touch with me, which was a bit of a godsend. You have to understand, I'd been trying to get hold of her for the past six months, but Regina's people are notoriously elusive. Back around Halloween she dropped by the office, and I showed her my new line of jogging gear."

"I take it she wasn't impressed," said Geneva, eyeing his garish tracksuit.

"What makes you say that? No, she loved it. I drew up a contract and she signed it right there in the office. And then, just after Thanksgiving... she backed out." Clyde massaged his hands irritably. "I don't think you know how much I had riding on this endorsement. Her pulling out jeopardized the whole future of the company."

"Did she give a reason?" Geneva asked.

"No, and that's what was so infuriating. I called her office repeatedly, hoping she might give an explanation, and she ghosted me. What had she heard? What was she upset about? I can't fix a problem if I don't know what the problem is."

Iris cleared her throat. "I'm not a huge businessperson, but isn't there usually a penalty when one party reneges on a contract? How did she manage to get away with that?"

"Being as famous as the Queen and having excellent lawyers, would be my guess," said Clyde in a contemptuous tone. "I wouldn't mind having that kind of power."

"It doesn't seem to have done her much good," said Geneva. "She's dead."

Clyde made an unconvincing attempt at looking mournful. "Anyway, I didn't challenge her on it. And I didn't kill her if that's what you're thinking."

"I'll keep that in mind," said Geneva, who had heard so many denials from murder suspects that she no longer paid them any mind. "But you had good reason to hate her—"

"I won't pretend I wasn't angry, but I think I was more baffled than anything. I spent the next week desperately trying to get an endorsement from Dolly, which didn't work out—you have no idea how hard she is to get hold of—"

"I've met Dolly, actually," said Iris, a statement that made everyone present turn in surprise. "Back in my twenties, my cousins and I used to visit Dollywood during the summers and sometimes she'd come out and chat with us. She's just about the world's nicest lady."

Geneva stared at Iris for a full minute, as if wondering why her best friend had neglected to mention this fact before now. "We'll come back to that later," she said finally, and turned back to Clyde. "You can't have been the only person affected by Regina's betrayal. Can you think of anyone else, maybe a disgruntled staffer—"

But before Clyde could respond, Geneva felt a firm hand on her back and a brusque man's voice said in her ear, "You three goons have been standing here long enough; make a purchase quick or I'll accuse you of loitering."

"We're not dealing drugs, if that's what it looks like," said Iris, unhelpful as ever. "If you'd just give us a minute—"

"I don't care if you're plotting to kidnap the president's daughter," said the manager, "so long as you buy something."

Iris grabbed a small bottle of champagne from the rack. At the same instant Geneva said, "George just texted me; he's waiting for us outside the fabricator's." She turned to Clyde. "Where are you living if we need to get hold of you again?"

"Lord willing, this is the last you'll ever see of me," Clyde replied, and grabbing a case of beer, he strode off to the counter.

[9]

Iris's car remained in the repair shop for the rest of the week, during which time she got around town with assistance from the women at work and from Hilda, who had turned back up looking profoundly if quietly embarrassed by the events outside the precinct on Saturday. It didn't seem to have occurred to her that stirring up a mob with demagogic rhetoric could result in unruly behavior.

"All I did was get them riled up," she said as she drove Iris to work on Thursday morning. "When has a mob ever hurt anyone?"

Geneva, meanwhile, went searching on social media for Blythe Bell and found her still living in Wrangler's Hill. By an odd coincidence, she was renting a room in a house owned by Emmett Hickinbottom, who worked as a sales rep for a well-known software company and lived in the same neigh-borhood as Regina Baldwin.

Geneva recalled with a painful twinge, Regina's suspicions that he was trying to poison her when she returned home at the end of the summer.

Unmarried and having no family of his own in the area, Emmett had begun renting out guest rooms in his colossal home in the hopes of picking up a bit of extra income, but at present, Blythe was his only tenant.

After exchanging some words on social media, Geneva and Iris rode over to Emmett's house on Friday night just as the sun was setting. George dropped them off; he was heading toward the library to write some poetry and promised to nip back over when they had finished.

"Don't let those suspects bully you," he told them, with the air of a mother addressing a child. "Remind them you could easily frame them for murder and throw them in jail."

"George, you *are* a darling," said Geneva, kissing him once on the forehead before she got out of the car.

Together, she and Iris strode up the drive toward the front porch. Iris rang the doorbell, and they waited. Dusk was falling and a cluster of birds with sleek, dark feathers had assembled on a power line on the opposite side of the street, beaks clicking as if to gossip about the newcomers. The Hickinbottom house bordered Regina's property. All the lights were off in the house next door, and the yard was beginning to look a little overgrown, patches of weeds growing up around a private well.

"I'll never understand people who drink well instead of tap water," said Iris. "We had a well growing up, and it stained my teeth a dingy red. I'll take the water with fluoride in it, thank you."

"I sometimes forget that we're only a generation or two removed from the outhouse—" said Geneva, but just then the door opened, and Emmett poked his ruddy face out.

"Ach, I suppose you'll be wanting to see the lady?" he said, and he led them downstairs into a den that had been comfortably furnished with a pull-out bed, an entertainment system, and a pink mini-fridge. Blythe Bell was seated on the sofa looking a little dejected. Geneva had the impression she had only reluctantly consented to being interviewed.

"Before you ask," she said by way of greeting, "I didn't kill that woman. I'm possibly the only woman in America who wasn't a fan, but I didn't kill her. That honor seems to have gone to someone else."

"I don't know if I'd call it an honor," said Geneva, feeling that the conversation was already getting off to a bad start. "But I believe you. In the words of Hercule Poirot, if you had really killed her, you would have to pretend you didn't hate her."

"What? That's brilliant," muttered Iris.

"No, I won't deny that I hated her for a long time," said Blythe. She was facing away from them at an angle, her knees tucked up under her chin. "And then I hated her for how much I had hated her. As I got older, I wanted to apologize, which is why I moved into this house—I had a vague notion that maybe someday I would work up the courage to knock on her door and beg forgiveness."

"Forgiveness for what?" said Geneva, with all the resolve of a priest administering confession.

Blythe scratched at her neck. "I did some truly terrible things when I was fourteen or fifteen. I wasn't a bully, really—except when it came to her. I just didn't *like* her, and I couldn't explain why. There was something about her..."

"Was it her race, her religion?"

Even Blythe didn't seem to know. "It started out as just a resentment. She was so good at so many things, it was infuriating. I stumbled on some books at an antique mall—I won't even tell you what was in them—but they seemed to prove that 'people like her' controlled the world, that they always had. Complete rubbish, I know, but at the time I was fourteen and paranoid and *looking* for a conspiracy theory to explain why I had been dealt such bad cards in life. That's what anti-semitism is at its core, a conspiracy theory..."

She fell silent, her long nails digging into the skin of her wrists. She looked as though she were trying to punish herself. Guilt seemed to have been gnawing at her daily for nearly twenty years.

"One afternoon, I had to stay behind after school to do some remedial work for Spanish. As I was leaving the west building, I saw her coming out of the gym. Something in me just snapped, I think. I ran after her, yelling. I called her a colonizer, a parasite, a Nazi. It was... vicious. And people saw it. They saw me running after her, swinging my purse. She looked terrified. I don't think I would have hurt her, but... I don't know. I don't like to think about it."

Iris placed a hand over her mouth. "How did Regina react to that?"

"She called out for help. Some kids came running. They led her to the assistant principal, where she told the whole story. My parents were called, and when they found out what I had been reading, all the racist books were confiscated. I was confined to my room for basically a year. I had a lot of time to think about what I had done—what a disappointment I was. The fear in Regina's eyes. It had been thrilling at first, knowing I had that much power. But when I came to my senses, when I realized I was just young and mean and gullible, it was sickening. I wanted to make amends, but of course, they had moved me out of school by that point. I didn't see her again until really recently."

Geneva glanced up at this. "You saw her? When?"

Blythe brushed a long strand of hair out of her eyes. "It was early one morning two or three weeks ago. I was heading to work. It was still pitch-dark except for a thin streak of gray in the sky just above her yard. Walking through the driveway, I noticed the silhouette of a woman standing at the edge of the property. It startled me."

"Just standing there?" asked Geneva.

"Standing over the well. Peering down into it, I think. I guess she was having trouble with her water system. It was the first time I had seen her since moving into the house. I didn't want to miss my moment. I called out her name—she flinched, looking slightly terrified. She stood there for a moment, frozen in place. I said, 'Listen, I don't know if you remember me, but... I'm really sorry. I'm sorry for everything. And... I think you're great.'"

"Did you give her your name?" asked Iris.

Blythe shook her head, her lower lip trembling. "No, I guess that might've helped." She laughed an odd, nervous laugh. "She didn't say anything. Just looked at me for a moment, probably really confused. I mean, I'm sure she has fans coming up to her in the street all the time, but they don't normally apologize. We stood there staring at each other while the eastern sky lightened. I got in the van and went on my way to work. That was the last time I saw her alive."

"How did you react when you heard the news?" asked Geneva.

"Not well, obviously." Blythe wiped a stray tear from her eyes. "It was Emmett who told me. I had been napping all afternoon and woke to the sound of what looked like a million people in the street. Her property was crawling with reporters. I texted him to ask if he knew what was going on. He said he had been at the marathon, and Regina Baldwin had passed away suddenly. He said the detectives suspected foul play. I knew then that I was going to be a suspect, that I might even go to prison. I suppose it's what I deserve. I don't know how to even begin atoning for that—I'll probably carry the weight of it with me always. But at least... at least I got to say sorry. Some people don't even get that."

She fell silent, tugging at a loose thread on the left sleeve of her shirt. She looked thoroughly depleted after that long confession, as if all the energy had been drained out of her.

Iris reached into her purse and pulled out the small bottle of champagne. "Here, I think you might need this more than I do." Blythe took it and cradled it pensively in her hands. "I understand feeling embarrassed, and that was a really terrible thing you did. But it seems like there ought to be a time for letting go."

Blythe looked faintly surprised by the suggestion. "Let go? Why would I do that?"

"Because you're not at all the same person you were at fourteen or fifteen. You've obviously done a lot of re-examining of your old hateful assumptions. You don't seem like the sort of person who would viciously attack Regina, or anyone else now."

Blythe considered this for a moment. "Maybe not," she said. "I just... I wish there was a way of knowing when you had atoned enough. When you were forgiven. Maybe I needed to hear it from her, I don't know. How do you make up for something so awful?"

Geneva didn't honestly know; for that she would have needed a psychiatrist, not a detective.

"Knowing that I'm capable of that," Blythe added quietly. "Knowing that that kind of evil exists inside of me... I wish there was a way to fix it. But I don't know there is. Something about me is broken, and there's no fixing it."

$$[\ 10\ ]$$

Geneva and Iris left the house.

By now, the last of light was fading. Geneva texted George and told him they were ready to be picked up. George texted he would be there soon; he had gotten into a snit with the other poet in the library over a biography of Charles Dickens "and now I'm begging the librarian not to throw us both out."

"Wait, I think I might know this librarian," Geneva wrote back. "Is her name Millicent?"

"Yes, how did you know?"

"Sweetie, I know all the librarians. I'll shoot her a text and put in a good word for you."

While Geneva was texting Millicent, Iris was gazing forlornly at the house next door.

"I wonder if we could sneak in and have a look around. You think the police have searched the place yet?"

"Hmm. She's bound to have gotten some hate mail," said Geneva. "I'll tell George we're heading over there."

But entering the house proved a more difficult challenge than they had anticipated, even with all their years of burgling experience. A sign advertising an expensive security system stood in the front window, and a motion-sensitive light illuminated the porch at their approach, nearly blinding Iris.

"On second thought, maybe this isn't such a good idea," said Geneva, raising a hand over her face.

"I don't see why not. We've broken into houses before."

"Yes, but Regina had *money*. I bet there are cameras set up all over this place, and the police are going to be covering every inch of surveillance footage now that she's dead. I know Gerry likes us, but even he wouldn't be able to help us if we were caught on camera breaking into a celebrity home."

Iris shook her head and muttered something about the injustice of a world where the police valued some properties more than others. Geneva wasn't listening, though; her attention had been drawn back to the house next door, where Emmett had just emerged and was setting down some heavy cardboard boxes on the front porch. A soot-black cat with large, dilated eyes rubbed quietly against his leg.

"I'll feed you in a minute, Fredo," said Emmett. "I just need to get rid of some things, first... now that those two old hags have gone... I thought they'd never go..."

Geneva nudged Iris and motioned for her to sink low into the grass. They watched as Emmett began carrying the first box to the end of the drive, still chatting amiably with Fredo.

"Can't say I'm sorry to see the woman dead," he was saying. "Little Miss Perky Ray of Sunshine. Always posting those idiotic Instagram posts about 'living your best life' and 'enjoying today while you have it.' Well, she don't have it no more, does she? Hee-hee-hee..." He made an odd, wheezing laugh. "I suppose you can only annoy the world for so long before the world hits back."

Geneva and Iris exchanged meaningful glances. Jogging back up to the porch, Emmett grabbed a second box and began heading back up the drive with Fredo in tow, hungrily meowing and not in the least concerned with Emmett's beef.

"This whole neighborhood is full of weirdos, isn't it? Regina the bestselling author of cheerful inanities... Freya wanting to know the depth of a standard private well... Well, after this past weekend there's one less weirdo in the world." He shook his head, smiling. "Whoever killed her deserves a medal."

"Sure doesn't *sound* like he killed her," whispered Iris.

"You sure?" said Geneva. "That's a brag if I ever heard one."

Emmett placed the third box with the others and went back into the house. Through his window, they could hear the sound of an electric can opener. Geneva waited a minute or two to ensure that he wasn't coming back out, then rose from the grass and began heading toward the pile, motioning for Iris to follow.

It was dark enough now that they had to use the light from their phones to see properly. Geneva breathed a quick prayer that he wouldn't glance out of the window and catch them, then gingerly opened the lid of the first box and peered inside.

What they saw didn't make any sense, not at first. Six cans of paint, arranged in loose rows, two of which had never been opened and three of which were nearly empty. The second box contained more , and the third contained a pile of large, rusted batteries.

Iris stared at the haul in confusion. "I don't get it—why was he trying to hide these from us?"

Geneva was beginning to get an idea. "You remember what Giles said, about the traces of mercury, copper and lead that they found in her system?"

"Yeah, what about it? Do batteries contain lead?"

Geneva typed the question into the search bar on her phone. She read the first result aloud. "Batteries may contain metals such as mercury, lead, nickel, cadmium and silver, which may pose a threat to human health—"

Iris stifled a gasp. "So he wasn't poisoning her with the coffee, he was poisoning her with *batteries* and *paint.*"

"Sure looks like it," said Geneva. "Now if we could just get a few decent pictures and then alert the police—"

But at that moment they were interrupted by a noise from the other end of the drive. Emmett stood in the dim yellow porch light, clutching a shotgun in both hands and gazing at them with a look of level contempt.

"I really thought I was done with you girls," he said calmly. "If you're not off this property in about four seconds—"

In a single swift stride, Geneva stepped into the street, pulling Iris alongside her. "We're not on your property anymore," she replied. "What are you gonna do?"

Emmett grumbled in annoyance something they couldn't hear. "I'd like you to explain why you were pawing around in my garbage like a couple of raccoons."

"We won't be in your hair long," said Geneva. "We're headed to the police to inform them that you poisoned and killed Regina Baldwin."

Emmett was so surprised by this news that he lowered his gun. "What proof?"

"Those discarded boxes full of old batteries, for one," said Iris. "Those cans of leaded paint—"

"How did you do it?" Geneva asked, a ghost of a taunt in her voice. "Were you slipping paint into her coffee?"

Emmett dropped the gun onto the porch. "Ladies, I don't have any clue what you're babbling about. I didn't love the woman, I'll admit that, but I didn't murder her, either, not with paint or batteries or... or coffee..."

Unconvinced, Geneva gestured to the boxes. "What's all this, then?"

Emmett laughed a nervous laugh. "My mother died about a month ago. She was an artist, a painter. When she grew too old to live alone, I set her up in my attic where she spent her final days working on her various projects. After the funeral, I went up there and started clearing out a lot of her old junk, things I had no use for. I'd been planning to take these boxes down earlier, but then you gals dropped by, and I got distracted."

Geneva looked to Iris, who shrugged as if to say, *Sounds plausible enough.* "What about the batteries?"

Emmett winced. "Yeah, I've been accumulating those for a while now. I felt weird about throwing them away—not what you'd call environmentally friendly—and when I called a guy to inquire about professional disposal and removal, you wouldn't believe how much he wanted to charge me. If I'm going to spend three hundred dollars, I should be *getting* something, not getting rid of something."

"What were the batteries *for?*" asked Iris.

"What were they for?" he repeated. "They're just... they're batteries. People use them, to charge things. Do I need to explain to you what a battery is?"

Something in his frustration convinced Geneva he was telling the truth. A pair of headlights had rounded the corner and was heading toward them, a white Buick. George began to slow as he neared them. Together the two women bundled into the warm car, eager to get out of the cold.

Geneva stuck her head half out of the open window. Emmett still stood on the porch, watching them with grim amusement.

"We'll be back," she said. "If you played any role in Regina's death—"

It was then that he said a curious thing. "I know who killed Regina, but I'll never tell you."

George pressed on the accelerator, and the car tore off into the night.

[11]

"Do you think he meant that?" asked Iris as they sped off. "About knowing the killer?"

"No, he's just being obnoxious," said Geneva. She hadn't much enjoyed the experience of having a gun pointed at her. "Men of that sort are always letting on that they know more than they do. If he knew the killer, why hasn't he gone to the police?"

"When have the police ever solved a crime in this town with someone walking in the door with information?" Iris pointed out.

George recounted the resolution of his tiff with the Other Poet (Millicent had begrudgingly apologized, though she had allowed the Poet to take home the Dickens biography—a victory which he had celebrated by accidentally spilling orange soda on it just moments later). George listened with interest as they related the altercation with Emmett in Emmett's driveway and the revelation of Blythe Bell's long ago hate crime.

"Here's what I don't get," said Iris. "She mentioned feeling this hatred toward Regina and not knowing where it came from. She thought maybe it was because she was Jewish, but she couldn't explain why that would make a difference. I've heard so many people say that."

"Irrational hatred toward people is sadly very common," said George as he merged onto the highway. "It's like a virus that has been perpetually mutating throughout history. If you go back and read things that were being written 3,000 years ago, they could have been written yesterday."

Geneva said nothing. She rather wished they could have silence for a moment, as she could feel an idea forming like a cloud at the back of her mind and needed some space and time to tease it out.

"See, I wish we had learned this stuff in school," said Iris. "Obviously we read *The Diary of Anne Frank*, but I always assumed that was a one-time event. I didn't know this was *always* happening."

"No, it's a very mysterious and horrible thing," George replied. "People have been treating them this way for nearly their whole existence as a people. They were expelled from England in the 1200s and Spain in the 1400s. During the Middle Ages, they were forced to live in ghettoes and wear yellow badges... were forbidden from marrying non-Jews... during the Black Death, they were accused of poisoning wells and attacked by bloodthirsty mobs, because they had better hygiene and sanitation practices..."

Geneva, seated in the back, glanced up in surprise. "Wait, go back... say that again, what you just said."

George looked faintly pleased that someone was listening. "Oh, they were losing fewer people to plague because they washed their hands regularly, a habit which the rest of the world—"

"No, no... that's not it. If I could have just a moment's silence...."

George shrugged, looking a little offended. Isolated bits of recent conversations were beginning to assemble themselves in Geneva's mind... It was like seeing a puzzle neatly laid out. Emmett saying to the cat, "The whole neighborhood is full of weirdoes, isn't it?" Blythe, seated on the sofa in the den, saying, "I noticed the silhouette of a woman standing at the edge of the property... standing over the well..."

She opened her eyes with a start.

"George, we have to go back."

"I agree," he said solemnly. "I wish we could undo the centuries of hate—"

"No, I'm not talking about that, right now," she cried. "I'm sorry, I don't mean for you to feel like a taxi, but I need you to drive us back to the house we just left."

"Wait, why?" asked Iris, face creased in apprehension. "Did you forget your keys?"

Geneva shook her head. "No, because unless I'm wrong—and I'm almost never wrong—Emmett Hickinbottom's life is in grave danger."

Geneva asked George to stop the car about a hundred yards from the house. Together, she and Iris emerged from the car and crept through the bitter cold toward the trash-strewn drive.

Night had fallen and the first faint stars shone overhead through a diaphanous haze of cloud. In the house at the end of the drive, all was quiet save for a rustling of curtains in an upstairs bedroom. But as the women neared the house Geneva thought she heard, in the stillness, a frenzied muttering of voices. It lasted only a second or two and then subsided.

"What are we supposed to say when he opens the door?" asked Iris. "'Sorry to bother you again, we know we just accused you of committing a murder, but we think somebody might be trying to kill you?'"

Geneva shook her head. "We're not going through the front door." She pointed one finger discreetly to the rooms upstairs. "Listen."

Iris fell silent. Nothing at first—and then she heard it: a woman's voice, low but insistent.

"I don't want to do it, and I won't, if you promise me—*promise me*—"

"Blythe?" whispered Iris. Geneva motioned for silence.

"I told you, I can't make any promises," said Emmett. He was standing close to the window in the stairwell, and they could hear him clearly. "You know it's illegal to obstruct an investigation by lying to the police? And if I'm placed under oath—"

"Don't make me do it," came the first voice again, "so help me... I've already killed once..."

"Not on purpose," said Emmett with repressive calm. "If you kill me, you'll never see the outside of a cell again."

Geneva had heard enough; they were wasting time now. "We'll enter through the back," she said quietly. "They're distracted enough at the moment that they likely won't even hear us."

They were scurrying around the side of the house to the back patio when it happened—a single shot rang out. Badly startled, fearing they were already too late, Geneva slipped in through the back door with Iris following just a step or two behind. They found Emmett standing on the stairs, about midway between the first and second floors, eyeing a large hole in the wall beside him. A woman—Geneva recognized the voice now as Freya's—was screaming hysterically,

"Don't test me, I'll do it. The next bullet goes *through your skull."*

Freya was standing at the top of the stairs, hidden from view by the wall. Emmett, who had been facing the kitchen, raised one brow in surprise as the women entered. Geneva put a finger to her lips.

"Freya," said Emmett, his hands raised, "whatever problems you have now, I can promise you, they'll be a hundred times worse if you pull that trigger."

"I should never have told you," said Freya. She was in tears now. "I was so distraught when it happened, I needed to confide in someone... I *trusted* you..."

"And have I given you any reason to doubt my trust?" Emmett replied. "You haven't really told me much, just that you're to blame for her death, somehow. The police aren't going to arrest you based on my hazy recollections of a conversation we had on Sunday night when you were puking up Bacardi."

Geneva and Iris inched into the living room, their steps muffled by the thick carpet. Freya was standing just over them, still unseen.

"I heard what you said to those two women. 'I know who killed Regina, but I'll never tell.'"

"And I *won't*," said Emmett, unnaturally calm. "You have my word on that."

"But why even *say* that? You know it's just going to raise more questions. In another hour, your driveway will be swarming with cops—"

"Maybe it was a reckless thing to say, and I'm sorry. But it doesn't seem to have raised any suspicions, no one is beating at the door. In all likelihood, they've forgotten about it."

He stole a glance at the two women, who were now crouched near the door to the broom cupboard. Geneva had laid her phone on the floor, the better to record the conversation that was taking place overhead.

"Do you have any idea what prison is like?" said Freya. "My mother spent four years there. She said it was hell."

"You're much more likely to go there if you kill me," Emmett pointed out.

"I didn't kill *her*," Freya yelled. "That was never the intention. I'm no good with poisons, I... I should have been more careful."

"It was incredibly clumsy—I'll give you that. And now a woman is dead."

"That wasn't the plan, I swear," she said again.

"What were you trying to do, then? Because if you wanted to murder one of America's most beloved women, congrats. You succeeded."

There was a silence in which the January winds battered at the eaves of the house. Then, after an interminable pause, Freya began to speak.

"She wouldn't return my emails. I had been emailing her secretary for months, trying to warn her about the danger that climate change poses to all sentient life. Recently, I had begun following this channel on social media that exposed a massive conspiracy on the part of globalists to brainwash American students into believing that the earth isn't getting warmer. These big oil conglomerates are pushing a big lie, funding school textbooks and educational videos that say fluctuations in temperature are the result of solar winds and other natural factors. If the younger generation grows up believing this—"

Emmett, like Geneva, seemed to feel she was getting off-topic. "So you tried to warn her and she didn't respond. What then?"

"I needed to get her attention," said Freya, still holding the gun. "I attended one of her events in Waukesha and actually got close enough to shake her hand. I leaned close and said, 'Globalists are trying to brainwash American kids into thinking that climate change is a hoax.' She didn't know who I was, of course, but she *laughed* at me. Why would you laugh at that?"

Emmett didn't have a response.

"If there's one thing I can't stand, it's being ignored. If there's another thing, it's being laughed at. After the event in Waukesha, it was time to take drastic action. I rented a house just up the street from where she lived, which is how I met you. When she was away on vacation I slipped onto her property and introduced arsenic, lead and copper into the water supply. Haven't I already told you this?"

"And you didn't think that would kill her?" asked Geneva, incredulous.

Emmett turned to look at her. Iris turned to look at her. Geneva placed a hand over her mouth.

"Who's there?" demanded Freya. "Is there someone else in this house, and you didn't tell me?"

She swung the gun back around at Emmett, but Geneva stepped forward into her line of sight.

"Freya, it's all right," she said quietly. "I know everything. I heard everything."

Iris, perhaps feeling that there was safety in numbers, came trotting up behind her partner. "If you kill Emmett, you'll have to kill us, too."

Freya stood at the top of the stairs, just a few paces from the restroom. Her hair, which she had recently dyed an unnatural shade of blonde, was badly in need of combing. She glanced from Emmett to the two women as if taking Iris's challenge as an invitation.

"From everything you've told us," said Geneva, "it seems clear that Regina's killing wasn't premeditated. The smartest thing you could do is cooperate with the police and tell them what happened."

"I won't do it," said Freya, her eyes closed as though in prayer. "I won't."

"What was your endgame?" asked Iris. "Just to scare her?"

"I wanted her to get sick," Freya said slowly. "I know heavy metals can contaminate private wells through groundwater movement and surface-water seepage and run-off. I figured if she was bedridden with a mysterious illness for a few weeks, she'd take my warnings about irreparable environmental damage a bit more seriously."

"You do realize that was totally insane, right?" said Geneva.

"You do realize I could kill you right now," Freya replied.

Whether she would have followed through on her threat, though, they never learned. For at that moment, the door to the second-story restroom swung slowly and silently open and Blythe slipped out. In the palm of her right hand, she carried the small bottle of champagne, which she applied with generous force to the back of Freya's head.

It only took one blow: the gun fell from Freya's hand, and she sank to the floor, as still and silent as a stone.

$$[\ 12 \ ]$$

MUCH AS FREYA HAD IMAGINED, within twenty minutes, the street outside the house was crowded with puzzled neighbors, their faces flashing alternately blue and white in the light of police cars and ambulances. The blow hadn't killed Freya, who was only just waking and still badly dazed, calling for her late mother.

As Blythe told the story later, she had stolen up to the second-story restroom in search of the corkscrew which she had recently misplaced. While digging through the drawers she had heard yelling on the landing and, quickly deducing that Freya had a gun, had shut off the lights and texted a friend to call 9-1-1. For the next twenty minutes, she had listened in silence as Freya had admitted to killing Regina. When it became clear that she and Emmett weren't alone in the house,

Blythe had taken advantage of the distraction to sneak out and disable her—just as the first police car pulled into the driveway.

"This is going to sound so strange," she told Geneva, "but I've spent so much of my life brooding over Regina... when *that woman* told me what she had done, I felt the way you would feel if someone killed one of your best friends. I felt so possessive of her. I wanted to get revenge. And in a way, I think I did."

"I only wish Regina could have been alive to see it," said Geneva. "She'd have been pleased to see you defending her like that."

"It's a funny thing," said Blythe, turning away, "but sometimes you feel closer to someone in death than you did in life. Not to sound like one of those crazy ladies, but she's so close tonight I can almost... almost..."

Geneva reached forward and took her hand in hers. She'd had the same feeling, many times.

The marathon found a new host and was rescheduled. On the following Monday, twenty-three people appeared at the Wrangler's County Courthouse for a preliminary arraignment regarding the protests. At work and in church, the town seemed evenly split between those who felt that the defendants had acted appropriately in storming the precinct and those who wanted to forget that the whole incident had ever taken place.

On Wednesday the unwitting instigator of the kerfuffle, Mr. Mordecai Whistler, announced that he would be moving elsewhere. "This place is insane," he said in a written statement. "Only a fool would live here longer than it took them to pack their bags."

"And who's to say he's wrong?" Iris said when she heard the news.

On Saturday morning, George and Geneva and Iris met up for a celebratory breakfast at the Omelet Tree on Chartewell Street. What exactly they were celebrating no one seemed to know: in all the stress and fury of the investigation, both Geneva and Iris had been eating out rather more than they intended. But the murderer had been apprehended and Valentine's Day was nearing, which meant that spring was fast approaching—and that seemed reason enough.

"I've been thinking..." said Iris, taking a bite of artichoke. "What if I gave up writing mystery novels and switched to writing poetry?"

Geneva frowned. "Iris, dear, you've already invested so much time and effort in learning how to write whodunits. And crime fiction tends to sell, while poetry does *not*."

"No, but I think I could be really good at it," said Iris, with her usual unshakeable confidence. She motioned to a maple tree that stood across the road, in the parking lot of the new bed-and-breakfast. "I'll do it, I'll come up with a poem about that tree right now.

Bare branches grasp and snatch

Buffeted by winds and sleet but unperturbed

Like an octopus they seem to be reaching out

As if to grab some idiot."

"Better watch out," Geneva muttered.

Iris ignored this. "See, there's nothing to it. Just do that a couple hundred more times and slap a cover on it—within a year I'll be the new poet laureate. Maybe I'll be asked to speak at the next presidential inauguration."

"Isn't that the dream?" said George, who had written many verses of his own. "I can barely get my foot in the door of the local clubs to read my poems. Poetry is a shockingly cutthroat business."

"Well, if anyone can do it, I can—" said Iris. "Hey. Hey, why is everyone laughing?"

It was the best meal they had eaten in some time—which wasn't saying much, as the last week had been a fever dream of burgers and cheesesteaks. After about an hour, Geneva laid down her fork with a satisfied air. Outside the rain had just lifted and a light mist had settled over the plaza. The whole day stretched luxuriantly before them, in which they would run by the bookstore and maybe take a late lunch at the local park, given the unnaturally warm weather that week, and no one would bring up crime scenes or corpses or coroner's reports.

"Do you think we'll ever be anything other than what we are now?" asked Geneva drowsily.

"How do you mean?" said George.

"I just mean, we're all trying to become so many new things, late in life—you with your poems and Iris with her novels... is it really possible to reinvent yourself this late? Is it wise?"

"You seem to have re-invented yourself well enough," said Iris, jabbing the air with her fork. "Five years ago, you were an AP English teacher on the cusp of retirement. Now look at you."

"Fair, but even I can feel myself starting to settle," said Geneva. "This is probably who I'll always be, now—some small-time private detective dreaming of bigger things. Maybe we're all doomed to forever be chasing after things we can't have."

Iris studied her partner skeptically. "What sort of dreams could you possibly have, Gen?"

"Wouldn't you like to know," Geneva replied.

"I'll get my book finished, I *will*," said Iris. "And George will get printed in magazines and probably be invited to the White House. And you... you'll end up having your own TV series, like *Murder, She Wrote*, where Helen Mirren wins Emmys for playing you seven years in a row."

Geneva nodded thoughtfully. "Perhaps. But even if none that happens... isn't it a lovely thing, this life?"

They all agreed it was. George paid the bill and together, the three friends left the diner, glorying in the cool, fragrant weather and the promise of returning spring.

The End

CONTINUE READING...

Thank you for reading *Plots & Paranoia!* **Are you wondering what to read next?** Why not read *Crimes & Costumes?* **Here's a sneak peek for you:**

"I don't understand the youth today," said Iris Reeves, gazing darkly through the bay window. On the lawn across the street, a teenage girl lay dreamily in a hammock watching videos on her phone. "Every year I feel like they become more and more alien and strange."

"That's one of the reasons I quit teaching," replied Geneva Pomolo, her housemate, who was supposed to be filing her quarterly taxes but instead was seated at the kitchen table stalking dogs on Instagram. "They were beginning to reference things I had never heard of. I still don't know what a Justin Bieber is."

"You're better off not knowing," said Iris, who listened to pop radio at the office so that she could more easily follow conversations with her coworkers, several of whom were in their twenties and early thirties. Iris had begun discovering gray hairs at the tender age of twenty-four, which had provoked an early midlife crisis. Ever since, she had been waging a lonely war against getting older: she taught a youth Sunday school class at church and regularly texted her young niece, Nanette, wanting to know what Kids Today were watching. (Ominously, the newly married Nanette no longer seemed to have any clue.)

"I keep hearing about this—I think it's a website, or a TV channel—that all the kids are watching," said Geneva. "It's called TokBits. Have you heard of it?"

Iris froze in the act of making herself a margarita. "Yes, Wendy is constantly talking about it." Wendy was a friend who worked alongside Iris in the municipal water department. "It's sort of like PicTalk, only a bit more obnoxious."

This meant nothing to Geneva, who had only a hazy knowledge of PicTalk. "What time does it come on?" she asked, brushing a springy gray curl out of her eyes. "Maybe we can watch it tonight when George gets home."

"It's... not a show," said Iris, placing the margarita mix back in the refrigerator. "You'd have to download it onto your phone."

Geneva had only recently learned how to download apps onto her phone from her friend Suzie Orleans, whom she had sponsored in high school and who was now finishing her first year at Wrangler's Hill Community College. "So if I go to the app store, it should be—"

Iris shook her head, looking troubled. "I feel like I should warn you: when I said TokBits is a bit obnoxious, I meant *really* obnoxious."

Click Here to Continue Reading!

https://ticahousepublishing.com/cozy-mystery.html

Donna Muse has been a mystery buff for years! But she hasn't been a fan of blood and gore. So when the Cozy Mystery genre came into being, she jumped on board with both feet. She loves the amateur sleuth and is fascinated by the intense and often comical way the perpetrator is revealed. Donna lives in Maine with her husband, loves walking by the surf, fishing for striped bass, and playing with her grandchildren and her cats.

contact@ticahousepublishing.com